Gram Makes A House Call

Written and Illustrated by Christine Borders

Gram Makes a House Call

Copyright © 1999 by Christine Borders

All rights reserved.

First Edition

Illustrations by Christine Borders

Library of Congress Catalog Card Number 99-62955

ISBN 0-9671160-0-7

Printed in the United States of America
at Morgan Printing in Austin, Texas

This story is written in memory of my mother,

Camilla Karem, who came from Besharrey, Lebanon,

to the United States to live and raise her family.

She was tough, gutsy, loving, and giving

—strong physically and mentally.

Her family was her life.

This book is dedicated to

Carmel Borders,

without whose tenacity and

encouragement it would never

have been completed.

Chapter One

Rafe had the blahs.

He sat by the window hoping Chippie would call him to come play. Dusty climbed up into his lap, and Bud meowed jealously. Rafe felt better stroking Dusty as he watched the cold rain fall against the window. He decided to make a salami

sandwich to soothe himself till his mom came down. Suddenly she called from upstairs.

"Rafe, come up here. I want to talk to you." She didn't sound too good. Rafe hurried upstairs and forgot all about the sandwich.

He stood at the door of her bedroom. His mom was putting things into a small suitcase on the bed, and another large one was packed on the floor. She was crying. He had an awful feeling in his stomach as he said, "What, Mom?"

"Honey, you remember I told you we were going to have a new baby around here? Well, the time is now, oooh!" She bent over and held her side.

Rafe stumbled over the suitcase when he ran over to her. He fell on the bed. She hugged him and said softly, "Don't worry. Mothers always cry when new babies come. It hurts, but you always forget about it real fast."

Rafe felt sick. He didn't want her to cry or hurt. She was so swollen and uncomfortable looking. She was still putting things into the suitcase. He watched her, feeling miserable.

"Gram is coming now. Daddy is bringing her. She is going to stay with you and Dusty and Bud. Remember, I told you before?" She sniffed and blew her nose.

"I know you are going to be great and help her do everything."

He nodded. He felt mixed-up and scared. He never saw her cry much. She smiled most of the time. When he came home she smiled, and she smiled when he went out, when she fixed dinner, when he went to bed. She smiled a lot. But now she was crying. He felt awful. He sure didn't want a salami sandwich anymore.

He didn't much want a new baby either if
she had to hurt and cry about it.

She was such a nice mother. Besides
smiling a lot, she hardly ever yelled at him.

She would stoop down and talk low and soft to him even when she was mad. Then she didn't smile. Except lately she didn't stoop much. Come to think of it she didn't smile so much either. Rafe was trying hard to be tough and not cry. He wiped his nose on his sleeve and she sat down beside him on the bed. Dusty and Bud climbed up too like they wanted to be in on everything.

"Rafe, I'm going to the hospital now to have a new baby. Our family will soon be four people and two cats. You take care of Gram till I get back, and don't you worry. It will be over fast and I will be home with you and Daddy like always. Oh!" This time she bent over farther and cried harder, and

Rafe cried and hugged
her. Dusty and Bud
meowed
something
awful.

He heard the
truck out front.
His daddy
came charging
up the stairs
two at a time and
fell over the suitcase and landed on the bed
with all the rest. The cats ran away and hid
under the bed.

"You okay, honey? You ready? What
should I do?" Daddy's voice sounded
strange and shaky.

"Yes. Yes. We better hurry. Where's Gram? Honey, bring the suitcase. Rafe, good-bye, sweetheart, be good to Gram and don't worry."

Daddy jumped up from the bed and fell over the suitcase again. Even Mom laughed. He picked up the little suitcase and the big one and helped Mom down the steps, Rafe following with Dusty and Bud.

Gram was hanging up her jacket. She had on her navy blue sweater that she always wore. Rafe's Gram was different from any other grandmother in the world. She talked different and looked different. Nobody had a grandmother like her. Her cheeks were rosy, and she was very excited. They all went out on the porch.

The rain had stopped. Mom and Gram hugged and cried. Daddy helped Mom into the pick-up truck and threw the suitcases in the back. He jumped into the driver's seat and jumped out just as fast. He ran back up onto the porch.

"The keys! Rafe, help me find the keys!" he screamed.

Everyone ran in all directions— cats, Gram, Daddy, Rafe. Mom was bent over crying in the truck. It was wild!

Suddenly, Rafe ran down from upstairs shaking the keys. Soon the truck was gone down the road, squirting mud from the puddles the rain had left.

Gram and Rafe sat on the top step of the porch for a long time. She had her arm around him and they both had wet eyes. The sun was making everything pink and orange as it said good-bye for the day behind the little church steeple over in town.

Chapter Two

"Gram, how long does it take to get a baby?"

Gram carried her cane with her wherever she went. She poked at Dusty with it. She didn't really like cats, even though she always gave them scraps to eat.

"You can't tell, Rafe. Sometimes long, sometimes not so long." Gram came from another country outside of town, outside of the United States of America. Rafe couldn't remember the name but he knew it was a million miles at least and over the ocean. Gram talked funny and Rafe loved to hear her say words like "butnus" for buttons, and "tullyphone" for telephone.

"They will call us on the tullyphone when the baby comes."

They went inside and Gram kept the cats out with her cane till the door was closed.

Rafe had a stupendous appetite, and when Gram came he was in heaven. She made food different—no sandwiches, although he liked sandwiches, too. She would go outside and gather up little green things that grew wild and clean them for hours and cut them up in a salad that was so good it made your heart sing.

She began to rattle Mom's pots and pans and Rafe knew something good was on the way. Soon they had cabbage rolls and some round flat bread that you could tear off in pieces. She made something she called taboolee in a big salad bowl. It had wonderful crunchy things in it along with some of the mint and parsley she got from the garden. When Rafe asked for more, Gram's face got shiny and pink with delight.

"*Sahtyne*, Rafe," she said. Rafe knew that meant she loved him, and that she was happy he liked her food, and that she hoped it made him grow strong and healthy and live a long and happy life, all in one word.

Rafe felt much better after he put away two plates full of the wonderful meal. He decided he would help Gram do everything till his mom got back, because she had to walk with a cane, and she said she couldn't hear anything. She wore funny thick glasses that made her eyes look real big, and she put her teeth in a glass of water when she went to bed at night.

"Gram, when Mom comes home, can you stay awhile?"

"Sure, Rafe. I stay and cook for you and your mom and dad."

"And the baby. Won't you cook for the baby too?"

"Not right away. The baby, he don't eat too much at first. He just drink milk," she laughed.

He put on his pajamas. Gram let her braids down, and put on a funny white cap that tied under her chin. She put on her nightgown and housecoat.

They played a loud game of "Jack Takes Them All," and Gram was very serious about winning. She yelped when she got a good hand, and banged her cane on the floor when she was losing. Rafe loved to win, and it ended up a very exciting time.

"We have to go to bed now, Rafe. Maybe they call us from the hospital before we sleep."

"I hope so, " Rafe said. She was covering him up and tucking him in. She couldn't read him a story. His gram couldn't read. But she told him some that weren't in any of his books. He loved them. They were about far off lands and other times.

Rafe dreamed about babies, and his mom and dad. They were in a big hospital full of babies who were in big bubbles hanging from the ceiling. They didn't know which one was theirs. Mom was crying and Dad was mad. It seemed like they were all mixed up for a long time, and they never did find their own baby.

The phone woke him up suddenly. He was glad the dream was over. Gram had the phone. She was waving her arm, and

her braids were swinging. Her cheeks were pink and she was saying, "Baby! How is baby? And mother? She is good. Thank the lord! Yes, Rafe is fine. Yes, I tell him. He is good boy. Yes. Good. Okay. You be late, come home to eat! Plenty to eat. Bye, bye."

Her cheeks were pink and her eyes were shining. She was happy. But Rafe couldn't understand some of her words because her teeth were in a glass on the dresser. Also, she was laughing and crying. She was hugging and kissing him. Dusty and Bud peeked out from under his bed. He hoped she wouldn't see them. They were supposed to be in the basement. They didn't come out. They knew Gram would send them down with her cane in a flash.

Rafe figured out from Gram's gasps and squeals that his mom had a baby boy. Rafe had a brother. His mom was feeling better. She had explained all this to him before, but he couldn't remember any of it. He was so glad that that she was feeling better. Maybe she wouldn't cry any more, and maybe she could stoop over and hug him and smile more, like she used to.

Chapter Three

Rafe didn't get to see his dad much that week. When Dad left his gas station he went to the hospital and came home after Rafe went to bed. Rafe missed him and his mom.

A couple of days later, just when he was feeling pretty sad, Gram announced they were taking lunch and going down to the creek.

"You can call Chippie to come. We got good lunch. Plenty to eat. Bring those dumb cats if you want, Rafe." She chirped, while she started banging pots and pans.

"Really, Gram? Oh, goodie! Can I really? Can I bring my ball and glove too?"

"Sure, honey," Gram replied.

Rafe yelped for joy and dialed the phone at once. Chippie could go. Rafe forgot about his mom and the baby for the first time in two days.

"Bring a towel and a table closs, Rafe. I'll make some hard eggs and slice some bunadoora."

Rafe knew that meant tomatoes. She hurried about the kitchen making a lot of noise slamming cabinets and pans. Rafe helped and before long they had a basket full of goodies and another empty basket for greens. Rafe took his fishing pole and selected some rocks from the driveway to throw into the water. Gram tied a scarf around her head and put on her navy blue sweater that she wore everywhere. She put the beads in her pocket that she prayed with all the time.

Chippie arrived about as happy as Rafe. He had a bag of cookies and a bat and ball and catcher's mitt. It was going to be a great day. Gram was loaded down and poking Dusty with her cane as the parade of grandmother, two boys, and two cats went out into the bright, shiny day. They were all smiles and looking forward to a fine picnic and a day outside in the fields by a pretty stream. They didn't dream how exciting it was going to be.

"Gram, maybe I can catch a fish. Won't that be fun?" Rafe babbled excitedly.

"Yes, fun. I cook it for supper. You catch, I cook," she promised.

Rafe and Chippie trotted on ahead, followed by the cats. Gram poked the cats with her cane when they got in her way.

Chippie didn't talk to Gram very much. She seemed strange to him. He wondered why she wore that scarf around her head and had a sweater on when it was 80 degrees. Also he couldn't understand much she said. It was funny, Rafe understood everything. Chippie felt a little left out but he always had a good time and the food was great. Rafe's gram always made him eat something even if it wasn't lunch time or dinner time either.

They took the turn farther away from the last houses till they came to the widest part of the stream. There were lots of trees hanging over the water, and a nice grassy spot flat enough to spread their picnic.

"Rafe, you and Chippie spread the table closs on de grass," Gram said excitedly.

"Okay, Gram. Can we eat now?" he chirped.

"Not yet. Too soon," she was putting her empty basket over her arm. "I go get some dumbie and nana down by water. Maybe some jarjeer. We eat pretty soon."

"Can we have a cookie?" Chippie pleaded.

"Sure. Yes. Have a cookie. Just one. We got good lunch," Gram called as she went farther on down the water's edge. She carried a small knife in her basket and was poking here and there with her cane, checking all the things growing along the water's edge.

The bright sun danced over the water. Chippie and Rafe saw some blue gill jump to the top of the water and make circles when they went back in.

"Let's catch one, Rafe. I see a million," Chippie got very excited.

"Okay, get the worms." Rafe was fixing the fishing pole.

Chippie produced a tin can of worms and they put two of them on hooks. Each had a pole.

"You go over there, and I'll stay here," Rafe ordered, and Chippie moved a little ways upstream. They could see Gram bent over pulling green things out of the ground with her little knife. Every so often she would straighten up and yell at them to be careful.

"Don't go so close to water. Too cold for swimming! Be careful!"

"Okay, Gram, we won't," Rafe replied, as they edged closer to the creek.

Some time passed. Everyone was pretty quiet. It seemed as though each was lost in their own thoughts. The birds were having a meeting in a big oak tree, chirping and chattering and flying in and out. Several

squirrels scurried here and there picking up bits of acorns and other goodies to hide. Lots of yellow butterflies fluttered around some buttercups close to the stream.

Chippie got a bite.

"I've got one, Rafe, I've got one. It's big too. Look Rafe! Look!" he screamed.

Rafe looked over at the fat sparkling fish, wiggling and twisting in the sunlight.

"He's huge," Rafe said grudgingly.

Chippie put the blue gill in the bucket and rebaited his hook. Rafe sat sullenly, hoping he would catch one twice as big. Gram was so far away now, she was like a speck down at the next bend in the water. He wondered where the cats were.

Suddenly he heard Gram scream! Chip

and Rafe dropped their poles and sped down to where she was.

"Rafe! Rafe! A snake! A slimy snake! Hurry, hurry!" Then she screamed some words Rafe had never heard before. A couple of times he heard a word that his mom had washed his mouth out with soap for saying.

She was beating the ground with her cane. By the time Rafe and Chippie got to her, she had demolished a long, yellow and brown water moccasin which lay dead at her feet.

"Gram, Gram! It's okay, Gram! You got him! Boy, you really got him!" Rafe yelled, as he looked at her in admiration.

"Wow!" said Chippie.

"He crawled between my legs! Of all the nerve of him!" Gram screamed whacking the dead snake with her cane once more for good measure.

"Wow," said Chippie.

Rafe picked up her basket. "Come on, Gram. Your basket is loaded. Let's go back and eat."

"Eat! I can't eat! I'm sick. That ugly snake take my appetite. No food for me. You and Chippie can eat."

Chapter Four

Rafe carried her basket, and she
walked back to the picnic site, red faced

and puffing. Chippie trotted along trying to keep up with Rafe and his Gram. Her face was red and she seemed awfully hot, but she never took her scarf or sweater off. She was saying some strange words which Rafe seemed to understand. Chippie never heard such strange sounds. He wished he knew what she was saying.

Everyone was much calmer when they got back to their spot. Chippie showed Gram his fish, and she was delighted.

"You catch a fish now, Rafe. We will have enough to make supper and Chippie can stay and eat."

They lunched on hard-boiled eggs, sliced tomatoes and some kind of cold meat rolled up with some of Gram's chewy bread.

Chippie watched them and decided he would try a strange rolled-up sandwich. He found it to be delicious. Gram had evidently forgotten she was sick and ate two of the sandwiches and two tomatoes and even tried a couple of Chippie's cookies.

After lunch, the boys threw their baseball a while, then went back to fishing. Chip caught another blue gill. Rafe was almost ready to cry when something tugged at his line.

"Chip! Chip! I got something. Help me! Hurry! It's big."

Chip ran over and they both held on to the pole. It bent down toward the water. They thought it would break. Finally, they could see a lovely, frisky, shiny, stupendous bass. It wiggled and jumped around for a long time. After an endless struggle, the two boys got it off the line and into the bucket. It barely fit.

"Gram, Gram. Come see!" Rafe hollered.

She was already on her way back from collecting her special greens. She had gone almost as far as she was before. Evidently, she forgot all about the snake. She had emptied her first basket of greens into the table cloth, and had the second basket almost filled.

"Beautiful! Good to eat! Dee lishus," she exclaimed, squeezing Rafe and kissing him till he was breathless. They all stood around admiring the slippery, sparkly fish for a long time.

"We be going home now, boys. We have a lot to carry." Gram was already picking up and packing up.

Rafe picked up the bucket with their fish and found it to be pretty heavy. He dragged it along for a while when suddenly he slipped on some wet stones and toppled over smack into the water, making a big splash. The bucket of fish turned over in the grass.

"Rafe, Rafe," Gram screamed. Chippie tried to reach Rafe's hand to help him out but he couldn't reach him. One of Rafe's shoes was stuck between two rocks under the water. Gram was hysterical. She screamed a lot of funny words. She moved

as close to the edge as she could. She held her cane out to Rafe and she and Chippie pulled on it as hard as they could. They tugged and tugged. Rafe got a better hold on the end of the cane and all at once came right up on the bank.

"My baby! You are wet and colt! We hurry home now. I gif you hot bath and hot tea!"

Gram was wiping him off and drying his hair and ears on her apron. Rafe was kind of embarrassed in front of Chippie because she was making such a fuss over him. Besides he didn't like Gram's tea.

She crammed all of her greens into the baskets and wrapped Rafe in the table cloth. He didn't want it wrapped around him, but didn't say anything because of all that had happened.

They were ready to go after putting the slippery fish back in the bucket and adding water. Then, Rafe remembered the cats.

"Gram, where are Dusty and Bud?"

"I dunno! Those darn cats!"

"Gram, we have to find them!"

Chippie stopped suddenly and said, "Listen!"

"Meow. Meow."

"Hear that?" Chip said, taking off in the direction of the sound.

"Meow. Meow."

They all followed. They found Dusty and Bud way up in a maple tree looking down at them innocently. Dusty, a plain little gray cat, jumped from one limb to another and landed at Gram's feet. She poked him with her cane angrily.

"You come down here! Bud!" Rafe tried to sound stern.

Bud was a Siamese cat and very much a sissy. But he was so gorgeous everyone was nice to him. He did not budge. He just looked at them with his beautiful blue eyes.

"Come down here, this minute, you dumb cat! Can't you see this poor baby is wet and colt," Gram yelled.

Bud wouldn't move. Gram took her cane and reached it high into the tree and hooked it around Bud. Carefully she moved him down to the next limb. Then

to the next and finally to the ground.
She poked him with her cane good this
time.

Finally they had everything together: two
baskets full of greens and leftover food, one

grandmother, one wet boy, one dry boy, two cats, and three fish in a bucket.

Chapter Five

They trailed back along the creek, back toward all the houses on their street, and finally home. They were all tired after a very exciting picnic, to say the least.

Gram took the fish out back and cleaned them. Dusty and Bud meowed like crazy until she finally threw them some scraps from the fish. They nibbled and chewed and looked around to be sure nobody else got any. They seemed very happy.

Gram brought the fish in all clean and pink and silvery. She put them in salt water, then sat down to clean her wild greens. Chippie skipped through the kitchen and announced that he could stay for dinner.

Gram said fine and went on cleaning the greens.

Chippie ran outdoors and found Rafe.

"What is she going to do with all those

weeds?" He asked.

"Those are not weeds, silly. Those are greens. Gram cooks some of them in a pot, and they are yummy."

"Yuk," said Chip. "They look like weeds to me."

"S'all you know. Gram could get lost in the woods and never get hungry. You will change your mind after you taste her greens."

"Yuk," said Chippie.

That evening they all sat down to a very interesting dinner. They had fresh fried fish and a big pot of greens, a platter of lentils and rice, and a big salad with some of Gram's greens in it. Chippie didn't want Gram to know he didn't want any, so he tasted some of the salad and took a second helping. Rafe enjoyed everything as always.

"Eat some mmjudra, Chippie," Gram offered.

"Huh," said Chippie puzzled.

"This, dummy," and Rafe passed the lentils and rice.

Chippie wanted to say no, but Gram was watching and he took a little. He ate a bite, then another. Soon it was gone, and he wished he had more. Gram saw his empty plate and replenished it for him.

"*Sahtyne,* Chippie."

"Huh."

"*Sahtyne.*"

"Ma'am?"

"Never mind," said Rafe. "I'll tell you later." Rafe didn't much want Gram to use that word on Chippie.

After the fine meal, Chippie and Rafe took out the garbage and fed the cats,

who were not too hungry after their afternoon treat.

The phone rang. It was Rafe's mom. After Gram screamed into the phone for a while, Rafe got to talk to her.

She wasn't crying. She didn't sound swollen. She was smiling. He could tell. She sounded like she could stoop over and touch her toes. Rafe was so excited, he had to go to the bathroom fast. He gave the phone back to Gram.

His mom was coming home in two days and bringing his new brother. He had no idea what to expect, even though his mom talked about it to him for weeks before. He wondered what his brother's name was. Would he just call him brother? Could he throw a baseball? Go fishing?

After Chip's mom came to get him, Rafe fell asleep exhausted on the floor. He didn't know how he got to bed, but he had another crazy dream about babies, and snakes and cats. He woke up crying. Gram was holding him and kissing his forehead. She took him to the bathroom. Then he fell back to sleep and did not dream anything.

Gram spent the next day cleaning up the house and washing everyone's clothes. Rafe helped some. He put socks and their mates together. Then he played outdoors with the cats and rode his bike to Chippie's house.

Chippie's mother was very excited about Rafe's new brother. She asked Rafe a lot of questions that he couldn't answer. He promised he would find out everything and let her know. She gave him a cookie. He felt important. He felt very good.

On his way home, Mr. Hale, the mean old man two doors from Rafe's house, was in his yard. Usually, he yelled at Rafe about something. Today he said, "Hello Rafe. How's your new brother?"

Rafe was astonished that the mean old man sounded so nice.

"He's fine I think," he stammered.

"Good. Good. I guess he'll be coming home soon," said the not-so-mean old man.

Rafe went on, and the mailman was putting mail in their mail box.

"Hello, Rafe! How's the new brother? How big is he? What's his name? When is he coming home?"

Rafe loved all of the attention. Everyone was very happy and excited about a new baby. Maybe it wasn't so bad after all.

"Pretty soon, Mr. Mailman. Maybe tomorrow. We are getting all ready," Rafe said as he rode his bike around the back.

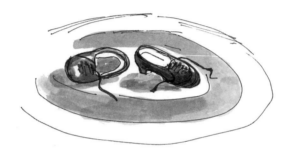

Chapter Six

Gram told Rafe to get ready. She
wanted him to go downtown with her. She

needed to go to the bank and the grocery. He knew his Gram would buy him a prize. She always did. Almost.

Gram had the house all shiny and clean. Rafe didn't wash his hands because he was afraid he'd mess up the sink. They left the cats in the basement and locked the front door and left.

The walk to town wasn't long. Gram had her scarf and sweater on. She looked hot. She walked briskly. Rafe pulled the wagon to carry the groceries they would buy. Her cane made a rhythmic sound on the sidewalk. She didn't seem to need it much that day. Her cheeks were rosy and she was excited. Rafe kept up with her pretty well. They talked all the way.

"Gram, what's the baby's name?"

"Gabriel. Gabriel. Beeooteful name, huh, Rafe?"

"Do I have to call him Gabriel?"

"Well, I not know. Maybe they let you call him Gabe."

"How much does he weigh? Is he big as me?"

"No, no, baby is small. You can carry him in your arms."

"Really, Gram? Gosh, will he break?"

"No. No. He is strong. He will grow fast and be big boy for you to play with soon."

"I miss Daddy. I haven't seen Daddy for a long time."

"You will see him tomorrow. He bring your mother and baby home tomorrow.

You will have big family, Rafe. You be big brother, then. You have to take care of your mother and baby for a while. Also those dumb cats."

"We go to bank first." They turned down Main Street toward the bank. There didn't seem to be much going on that day in the little town. The street was pretty empty.

Suddenly, a loud buzzing sound scraped through the air. Gram and Rafe looked around to try to see where it came from. It seemed to come from the bank. They heard the sound of breaking glass, and something that cracked like shots. Rafe hid behind Gram's skirt. She looked around trying to figure out what was happening. They were just two stores away from the bank. Suddenly, a man came running out of the bank headed straight in their direction.

Gram stood her ground. She never moved. The man carried a cloth sack and a gun. Gram just stood there. He was coming straight toward them. Rafe started to cry. He hid behind Gram. The robber carried a

gun, and just as he ran past them, Gram
stuck her cane out and caught his left foot
as it was coming down. He crashed into a

parking meter. The cloth sack and gun flew into the air and money flew everywhere. The man hit his head when he fell and he was out cold. Gram never moved. She had watched the whole thing and the only thing she moved was her arm to stick out the cane. Policemen came from all directions. People screamed and sirens wailed. Rafe couldn't talk.

"Let's go to the grocery now, Rafe," Gram said above the noise.

They took off in the direction of the grocery, avoiding all the commotion. On the way, Gram didn't say very much. He thought she would be screaming. She wasn't. She was so quiet it was scary.

"Gram, you all right?"

"Yes. Yes. I be all right."

"Gram, you tripped the robber. You caught him right on the shin."

"Sush! Nobody see that but me and you, Rafey."

"I want to tell Charlie, the policeman."

"No. No. Don't tell. We keep big secret, me and you. Okay. We no tell. They make big noise about it. We got new baby coming. We don't need big noise. Okay!"

"Okay, Gram. Wow! You tripped him so clean. He didn't know what happened to him."

"I hope he don't," Gram said as they entered the grocery. Her face was blood red and her eyes were pressed together like she wanted to holler and was holding it back.

That night they heard about the bank robbery on the radio and not a word was said about how the robber got tripped and knocked out. They just said he was captured and taken to jail.

Chapter Seven

Next day Rafe's mom and new brother came home. Rafe couldn't believe how his mom looked. He knew for sure she could stoop over and touch her toes. His dad was very excited. He and Gram were running into each other trying to help. Gabriel slept through all the noise.

Gabriel looked different than Rafe had imagined. He was pretty red looking, and he didn't have any hair except a little fuzz. Rafe crawled up on the bed for a good look. He took one little hand in his and stuck his finger in between the baby's fingers. The baby held it tight.

"Mom, he's holding my hand. He likes me. He knows I'm his brother."

"Course, he does, honey."

Rafe ran out to find Chip to tell him the news. He couldn't find him anywhere.

He ran back upstairs to check on his brother. His mom was sitting in a rocker nursing Gabriel. Rafe stopped dead in his tracks. He was amazed. He remembered she told him something about that, but he didn't expect to see it actually happening.

"Whatchoo doing, Mom?"

"I'm nursing Gabriel, Rafe. It's time for him to have lunch."

"Can't he have a salami sandwich?."

"No, he can't. All he needs is this for a while."

"Whatchoo got in there?"

"Milk."

"Have you got orange juice in the other one?"

"No, honey. I guess that would have been too much to figure out."

His mom's face broke up into one of her best smiles. Then she threw her head back and laughed. She looked so young and skinny. Not swollen at all. Rafe was very happy.

Gram stayed a couple more days. Gabriel cried sometimes. They were always changing his pants and giving him baths, and washing his bottom, and putting cream and powder all over him. Rafe was glad he wasn't a baby. He helped a lot running up and down steps and getting this and that. He got to eat in

the bedroom with his mom twice. Best of
all his dad put him to bed.

Gabriel wasn't growing as fast as Rafe
hoped. He decided he would have to play
ball with Chippie till Gabriel got up out of

bed and came outside with him. He didn't know how long that would be.

The morning came when Gram was going home. She was cooking up a storm. She wanted them to have plenty to eat all week. She banged cabinets and pots and pans all morning. The kitchen smelled heavenly. There were several pots on the stove and bowls of fruit and vegetables on the table. All colors.

So much had happened in the last few days that Rafe couldn't believe it. He wanted to tell the robber story to somebody so bad. He thought he would burst if he didn't get to pretty soon.

Dad came to take Gram home. She had on her sweater and scarf. Her cheeks were pink and she smelled like garlic and onions. When Rafe hugged her it made him hungry.

"Good-bye, Rafey. Take care of your brother. He be big soon and go fishing with us."

"Bye, Gram. Thanks for cooking for me."

"Sure, honey. I be back soon."

She started towards the door. Suddenly, she stooped down and whispered in his ear. "You can tell you mom and dad about the robber if you want to now. Tell them no tell anybody else. It be family secret."

"Oh, really, Gram? Oh, Great. Okay, big secret!"

"Bye, Rafe."

"Bye, Gram."

They hugged again.

"Oh, Gram."

"Yes, Rafe."

"Don't forget your cane."

THE END

CHRISTINE KAREM BORDERS of Louisville, Kentucky, has been drawing and painting as far back as she can remember. She is the mother of seven children, grandmother of twenty-two, and great grandmother of seven. She has just turned 59. Again.

She is a self-taught artist who has had her work exhibited in art galleries throughout Kentucky, but she loves her role as grandmother best of all and has a full-time job keeping track of all those kids.